Sophie G Wanderlin

One of a Kind

Written by
P. J. Jackson

Illustrated by
Doyle Holz

Sophie G Wanderlin

One of a Kind

Written by P. J. Jackson

Illustrated by Doyle Holz

AuthorHouse™
1663 Liberty Drive
Bloomington, IN 47403
www.authorhouse.com
Phone: 1 (800) 839-8640

Published by AuthorHouse 12/31/2016

ISBN: 978-1-5246-5433-7 (sc)
ISBN: 978-1-5246-5432-0 (e)
ISBN: 978-1-5246-5431-3 (hc)

Library of Congress Control Number: 2016920600

Print information available on the last page.

Any people depicted in stock imagery provided by Thinkstock are models,
and such images are being used for illustrative purposes only.
Certain stock imagery © Thinkstock.

This book is printed on acid-free paper.

Because of the dynamic nature of the Internet, any web addresses or links contained in this book may have changed
since publication and may no longer be valid. The views expressed in this work are solely those of the author and do not
necessarily reflect the views of the publisher, and the publisher hereby disclaims any responsibility for them.

authorHOUSE®

to our
Future Generations

may you always be

Loving, Kind, & Respectful

Last night Sophie had a dream. A little voice told Sophie she was special. It said, "No one in the world is just like you. You are one of a kind. You have **"BIG IDEAS"** that matter. Your kindness can make a difference."

When Sophie woke up, she had a big smile on her face. Sophie felt different. Sophie felt special. Sophie decided that she would be happy and smile every day and ...

that's just what she did!

Sophie told BOB about her **"BIG IDEA"** to be happy and smile every day.

Sophie said, "BOB, let's go on a quest to make the world a better place. Where every day can be a new adventure in kindness" and ...

4

BOB purred.

The next morning, Sophie looked out the window with BOB. Sophie saw the sunrise. It started slow and small and grew big and bright.

"What an adventure!" Sophie declared. Sophie wished her mommy was there to see the sunrise.

The little voice in Sophie's head said, "You could draw Mommy a picture so she could see the sunrise too."
That idea made Sophie smile and …

that's just what she did!

When Sophie's mommy came home, Sophie gave her the picture and told her all about the sunrise adventure. Her mommy smiled and thanked Sophie for sharing. Sophie knew her **"BIG IDEA"** made a difference!

After dinner, Sophie told BOB about her **"BIG IDEA"** to draw a picture and share a memory with someone you love and …

10

BOB purred.

The next afternoon, Sophie watched television with BOB. A story about a storm showed people in trouble. Sophie wanted to help.

How can I turn this into my kind of adventure? Sophie thought. The little voice in Sophie's head said, "You could say a prayer and send love to the people in trouble." That idea made Sophie smile and …

that's just what she did!

Sophie closed her eyes and said a prayer. Sophie pictured the people in trouble getting food and blankets. Sophie pictured people helping people. Sophie knew her **"BIG IDEA"** made a difference!

Before dinner, Sophie told BOB about her **"BIG IDEA"** to pray for people in trouble and to send them loving thoughts and …

15

Puuurrr...🎵🎵🎵

BOB purred.

The next day, Sophie swung on a swing at the park. Sophie knew how it felt to be alone because BOB had to stay at home.

Sophie saw a little girl sitting all by herself. *How can I make today an adventure in kindness?* Sophie wondered.

The little voice in Sophie's head said, "You could go say hello and make a new friend." That idea made Sophie smile and …

that's just what she did!

19

Sophie and her new friend, Ellie, played all day. When they said good-bye, Sophie gave her new friend a big hug. Sophie knew her **"BIG IDEA"** made a difference!

When Sophie returned home from the park, she told BOB about her **"BIG IDEA"** to be kind and to make a new friend and …

BOB purred.

On Friday when Sophie came home from school, BOB did not greet her. Sophie started to worry about BOB. She looked under her bed. Sophie looked in the window seat – no BOB! Sophie did not know what to do. "How can I make *this* my kind of adventure?" Sophie exclaimed.

The little voice in Sophie's head said, "You could sit quietly. Close your eyes and think happy thoughts about BOB." That idea made Sophie smile and ...

that's just what she did!

Sophie sat down on a pillow and closed her eyes. Sophie took in a deep breath and then let it out. Sophie thought about BOB sitting on her lap. She thought about playing hide-and-seek with BOB.

Before Sophie knew it, BOB rubbed up against her knee.
Sophie knew her **"BIG IDEA"** made a difference!

Sophie was so happy to see BOB. Right away, Sophie told BOB about her **"BIG IDEA"** to sit quietly to make her worry go away and ...

BOB purred.

O n Monday, it would be Sophie's turn to bring a treat to school. Sophie asked her daddy if they could bake cupcakes over the weekend, and ...

that's just what they did!

When they were done, the cupcakes looked delicious. Sophie's daddy told her there were only enough cupcakes for the children in Sophie's class. Sophie wanted a cupcake.

The little voice in Sophie's head said, "You could take one. No one will know." That idea did *not* make Sophie smile. Sophie knew someone in class would go without a cupcake, and that was not her kind of adventure. Sophie wanted to do the right thing and ...

that's just what she did!

To be kind, Sophie knew it was important to bring enough cupcakes for everyone. Sophie walked away from the cupcakes and helped her daddy clean the dishes. Sophie knew her **"BIG IDEA"** made a difference!

Before bedtime, Sophie told BOB about her **"BIG IDEA"** of wanting a cupcake, but not taking one and ...

BOB purred.

All week, Sophie's **"BIG IDEAS"** were the best adventures in kindness ever! No matter the situation, Sophie always found a way to make the day her kind of adventure. Sophie wondered how she could continue her quest to spread kindness and make the world a better place.

The little voice in Sophie's head said, "You could share your **"BIG IDEAS"** with your friends." That idea made Sophie smile and …

that's just what she did!

Sophie invited her friends over for a campfire. She told them about all of her **"BIG IDEAS"**. Sophie asked her friends, "Could you make each day a new adventure in kindness too?"

Sy said, "Wow!"
Ricardo said, "How?"
The little voice in Ellie's head said, "We could do what Sophie does!"
Ellie smiled; she shared her **"BIG IDEA"** and ...

that's just what they did!

Sophie's friends promised to ...

Be happy and smile every day

Draw a picture to share a memory with someone

Be grateful and hug each other

Say a prayer and send love to someone in trouble

Be kind to someone and make a new friend

Sit quietly when worried and think happy thoughts

Do the right thing even when no one is looking

Sophie's kindness did make a *big* difference! Sophie told BOB about her friends' **"BIG IDEA"** and do you know what BOB did?

Bob purred.

Join Sophie and her friends on their adventures in kindness.

Ellie seems happy all the time, but she has a stormy side. How will Sophie help Ellie feel the sun when the clouds come?

Ricardo is a kind boy who would not hurt a fly, but at school he is being bullied. How will Sophie teach his classmates to take an adventure in kindness?

Mary Lacy is a big helper. When her Gramma gets sick, it seems too hard. How will Sophie help Mary Lacy cope with her Gramma's illness?

Tiffany loves to talk. When the things she promises are not getting done, there is a problem. How will Sophie help Tiffany learn that actions speak louder than words?

Raj is the new kid at school. When he gets in trouble he doesn't understand why. How will Sophie help others see that being different is okay?

Sy spends most of her time with a scowl on her face. It seems she is always upset about something. How will Sophie help her shift her energy toward good?

A positive energy like no other, PJ is one-of-a-kind! After three decades of influencing change in government, defense and aerospace industry, PJ is focused on mindfulness and our future. While working on the creation of Sophie G Wanderlin, PJ had a vision of twenty years into the future. She was on the stage again, but the audience wasn't a group of middle-aged engineers, the audience was twentysomething year-olds. They were all wearing rainbow socks, and they had grown up reading Sophie's adventures. Because of Sophie, these young people were loving, kind and respectful.

During the social marketing of her first book, *Adventure, Day One – Seven Positive Strategies When Life's Journey Gets Rough*, a tweet came across that read, "If you want to change the future, write a children's book". And that's just what she did! PJ promotes a positive self-image to create a culture of kindness from children to CEOs. A creative force that can influence culture change, Sophie G Wanderlin, BOB, The Cat, along with Sophie's friends, will make a difference and influence change in their own one-of-a-kind way! Follow Sophie on Facebook @SophieGWanderlin or contact PJ on Twitter @author_jackson

Meet the Author
P. J. Jackson

A magic maker, Doyle was born with a sketchbook in her hand! Upon graduation, Doyle jumped into the graphic design industry, starting her own business. Now the happy mother of two young boys, and bonus mom of two teenage daughters, Doyle lives with her husband and children in the suburbs of Philadelphia.

Whenever the clock says 11:11, Doyle's wish is that she will always be the parent her children need. Doyle's greatest desire is that her life be used to help others heal and become who they were meant to be. Doyle uses her experience of trauma to set a living example that one can rise from the ashes to live a full and happy life. Doyle spends her days doing what she loves: being creative and artistic. Her passion has now manifested into illustrating children's books.

Meet the Illustrator
Doyle Holz

"To be selected as the illustrator for Sophie G Wanderlin is the catapult I've dreamt about since I was a kid," Doyle shares, "I am both honored and humbled to be this much a part of something so meaningful, that's going to have a great impact on future generations."

Parents' Guide

Sophie G Wanderlin is seven years old. She is an only child who lives with her mother and father. Her mother travels for work and her father works from home. Sophie wears rainbow socks because she loves the sky after a storm.

Sophie's companion is BOB, The Cat. He is a 20-pound, gray Maine Coon. Different from a friend, BOB is called Sophie's companion because he is always at her side, listening and supporting. Sophie trusts BOB in a very safe way – without judgement or criticism.

In the book, Sophie G Wanderlin, One of a Kind, there are underlying themes to help you reinforce positive behavior:

- Sophie is a "One of a Kind" adventurer, where every day is a new adventure in kindness. This allows children to equate adventure to kindness and to see being kind as fun and adventurous.
- Sophie has **"BIG IDEAS"** which she turns into actions. This concept is accented with bold lettering to bring attention to it and to encourage your child to come up with their own **"BIG IDEAS"**.
- Sophie's mantra is "Find a Way to Be Kind Today" This is a simple way you can bring up kindness at any time during your day. Make it a game, have your child find ways to be kind and then post those **"BIG IDEAS"** on the community page!

The story has seven sections. Each section of this book focuses on a color and a theme and each of Sophie's **"BIG IDEAS"** is about being kind:

Red – Kindness toward self. Sophie realizes she is special and her **"BIG IDEAS"** matter. Being kind can make a difference toward strengthening your self-esteem.
Orange – Kindness through shared feelings. Making a memory, sharing a memory.
Yellow – Kindness through doing. Sometimes doing can translate into prayers.
Green – Kindness through loving. Making a new friend and hugging them.
Blue – Kindness through silence. Introduction to meditation, kindness of spirit.
Indigo – Kindness through strength of character. Doing the right thing is kind.
Violet – Kindness through wisdom. Making a difference by sharing your **"BIG IDEAS"**.

These colors and themes are summarized at the campfire. You can print out the campfire promise for your child so they can do adventures in kindness like Sophie and her friends.

If the book is too long to read to your child in one sitting, you can break it up by color. One color every night, and then use extra sections as rewards.

CPSIA information can be obtained
at www.ICGtesting.com
Printed in the USA
BVOW10*2100160117

473625BV00006BA/13/P